I0679713

CARNAGE AT THE PETTING ZOO

POEMS

ISBN: 978-1-962072-15-1

Cover art & design by: Melissa M. Combs

Octave
Eight
PUBLISHING
∞

octaveeightpublishing@gmail.com

CARNAGE AT THE PETTING ZOO

POEMS

DEDICATED IN THANKS:

To the most incredible person
I have ever or will ever know.
They know who they are.
Thank you for always supporting me,
even when I didn't think you should.

And to *you*, reading this book. Thank you.

"There is no place so haunted as the human heart." – John Mark Green

"See, to live is to suffer but to survive well, that's to find meaning in the suffering." – DMX

"I should face the truth, I could calm the storm if I wanted to." – Royal Blood

"Vanity is definitely my favorite sin. Kevin, it's so basic, self-love; the all natural opiate."
– John Milton, The Devil's Advocate

INTRODUCTION ON TRAUMA

I am in no way any sort of expert on,
well anything, but specifically trauma.
I only know my experiences and how
I've dealt with them.

Much of the writing in this collection deals
with trauma in one way or another; be it
childhood, emotional, physical, relationship
or self-induced.

It is important to me that people know this is
cathartic for me. This is not a way to place blame,
to accuse, to drag anyone else down.
This is nothing more than me confronting and
dealing with my own issues. There is a chance
that while reading this, some people may think,
"hey that's about me". It's not. It might be about
something or some time that you were a part

of, but it's an important distinction to note that facing the trauma is overcoming it, not dwelling on it or blaming anyone for it.

Again, this is my *personal journey*. Yours likely differs wildly and you may need to deal with things differently or face things with a different approach. That is okay. However you need to face your issues and do what works for you.

DEAF TONE

We're sorry
No one is available
To take your call
To break your fall

Please
Hang
Up
Give
Up

And try
Try
Try
Try
Try
Try
Try
Again

DOG DAYS

Summer was ending.

"I'm so ready for fall" she said

I'm so ready for death, I thought

Relief from something. Something *new*.

MIXTAPE

My life is a mixtape

Track one: the thing I love because of my mother, who I don't speak to anymore

Track two: that one thing my father and I did together even when he was abusive

Track three: that song I hate to love because it reminds me of my first heartbreak

Track four: that summer trip my best friend's family took me on when we were kids

Track five: the way I hate that I like the smell of old, stale cigarettes because they remind me of my cousin's house

Track six: the scars I put on my arms because of how they made me feel about myself

Track seven: the movies I love because you loved them first

Track eight: the movies I hate because I cry
thinking of the past

Track nine: the places I can't go anymore because
of the sadness attached to them

Track ten: Suicide and how much it's taken
from me.

*My life is a mixtape, made up of all the things
ever attached to anyone I loved*

BOOK BURNING IS FASCISM

Its not the books they want to ban, no

Its the words from which they are constructed
Its the thoughts from which they are birthed
Its the dangerous ideas they contain

Its not the books they want to ban, no

Its the freedom, the feminism, the honesty,
the liberated sexuality, the radical concepts of
equality, the division of power, the elimination
of wealth inequality

Its not the books they want to ban, no

It's the intelligence, our collected wisdom,
our shared experiences, windows into other
ways of life
Its empathy
Its a bright light shining on their corruption
Its not the books they want to ban, no

It's your right to think
Its opposition to them!

SKELETONIN

As the sky turns to spring
My heart turns to fall
I long for the grey days
I long for the chilled wind
The crunch of leaves
Paper bats flocking in windows
Plastic pumpkins adorning stoops
The world alight with orange
The excitement of fear
Felt racing down every street
The world celebrates
A different kind of holiday spirit
Seeps into hearts
Like fun-sized candy bars fall into pails
Skeletons dance with demons
Melatonin flows like fake blood
As the days grow shorter
As we turn out the lights sooner
Huddled in the safety of blankets
Watching scary movies
Telling ghost stories
Dressing ourselves up as fear
To find joy in conquering fear itself
As the sky turns to spring
My heart longs for halloween

ALL THE THINGS THAT MAKE US GREAT

We should never fear to speak our minds
To open our hearts and share
There is more pain in withholding
There is more fear in being afraid
There is risk in being unwilling

In a world of darkness there is light
in a spoken mind.
Order springs from
spilling the chaos of emotion
Confidence can surge in opening uncertainties
There is no ill not made better by
Good conversation

Be it by candle light
Be it by moonlight

Be it wrapped in shadow or warmth of home

Over bottles
Over distance
Oldest friends
Or most recent of strangers
We should never fear to speak our minds

To voice our fears to divulge our secrets
Everything is wasted if kept to our selves
We are wasted if never shared

You are never alone
You are never the only one

We should never fear to share our minds
For within our minds are all the things
That make us great

Doubt and weakness and insecurity and fear
And hope and desire and dreams

All the things that make us great

I DIE AT THE END

I looked up and saw my life
Spread out wide before me
Colors and sound wound around
Mistakes and missteps and failures
Mixing with successes and achievements
Everything laid out before me

I saw myself a child
So full of hope and potential
I saw myself a teen
Wasted with anger and resentment
I saw myself now
Hopeless and lost
I saw myself with age
Unfulfilled and desolate

My actions lay spread
Like a convoluted web
Each branching off into what was
What could have been

What never was
Impossible to follow
Impossible to discern the right path

MAGNETIZE

I am Magnetic
To the problems of the world
The issues the opportunities
The tragedies the miseries
I am Attracted
To the conflict to the fights to the blood
The brawls the arguments the death
I am Violent
Towards myself towards my thoughts
My own mind beats itself to death daily
I am Craving
The horrible things that transpire daily
Feed it to me let me gorge myself on it
I am Manipulated
Not lying vicariously through tragedy
Wanting needing to be part of the horror
I am Fed
Yearly monthly weekly daily hourly
Live breaking footage of misery and pain
I am Angry
That we have allowed ourselves to live
like cattle before the slaughter

BADGES

I'm capable of making
My own bad decisions
I said
As if I were proud of them
As if I pinned them to my chest
Like merit badges earned
When I was in the scouts as a boy
This one is for lying
This one is for self-inflicted wounds
This one for drugs
This one for alcoholism
This one for dropping out
This one for infidelity
This one for petty theft
As mundane as
Knot tying
Rifle shooting
Camping under the stars
My own bad decisions

Merit badges
Reflecting my life

COME OUT

When I opened myself
Discovered myself
And shared myself
I didn't fear for anger
I didn't fear for hate
These things I know, they're familiar
Life-long companions
I know how to deal with them
I feared something new
I feared doubt from without
I was afraid
My sincerity
My genuineness
Would be questioned
That performances would be demanded
Proof be provided
I feared that no one would believe me
I was afraid that I didn't believe me
But when I did; when I showed myself
I realized it didn't matter
I believe in me
I know my authenticity
I'm certified by my self
And that was good enough
For me to believe
In me.

BAPTIZED

I was baptized in the catholic church
I had no say in the matter
I attended masses and youth groups
I had no weight in the matter
A den of thieves
A den of wickedness
A den of vile things
Invaders
Rotten crusaders
Child rapists, child rapists, child rapists
Pillaging our bodies
Pillaging our souls
Pillaging our hearts our minds
Pillaging our flesh
Damn the catholic church
Burn it to the ground
Salt the earth where it stood
End the misery
And the abuse
End the hypocrisy
God will forgive you
Preach to the children
God will forgive you
For my sins
I hope your hell is real
I hope you burn there for eternity

CLEAN WITH KEROSENE

Bathe it all in gasoline
Clean it all with kerosene
struck match and some gravity
Watch as life explodes in radiant glory
And laugh into the greyed sky
Dance in the ashes flying by
Soak in the air of a reset life
Refreshed and free from your self-containment
Demolition is construction with the will to be free
Only you can let it all go
Strength be your tinder and your fuel
Build the material into a funeral pyre
Sing in celebration as a world burns
Farewell to the past as the present gave way
When the ashes all settle and
The breeze blows them all away
Your gray becomes bright white new with flame
Lit from within
Your future this is

DEVIL

What face does the devil wear
When it faces you down in the dark
Who's face does the devil wear
When you feel it in the streets
Which face does the devil wear
When you see it in your dreams
Tell me what it looks like
Who's face the devil has
When it chases you
Out paces you
At a cross roads
On a street corner
In the shadows
Away from light
In deepest thought
In darkest dream
What face does the devil wear
When you look into the mirror

HAPPY HAPPY BIRTHDAY

Many happy returns to me
Many happy years
Many happy days
Many happy regrets
Many happy mistakes
Missteps
Misspoken words
Broken reflections
Shattered mirrors
Like cake on the floor for the pests
Year on year on year on year
Running in sand
Burying myself
Running in the sand of the hourglass
Churning
Until I can't breath
I've lost the sky
Each grain of sand
A weight
A moment
I'll never get right
Happy to you
And many more

UNKNOWABLE

I tried to help you realize
What I don't know myself
That while you plainly see me
I can't see myself
While you know me deeply
I don't know myself
While you love me endlessly
I don't love myself
While you want to understand
I can't explain myself
And while you tried to help me
I can't help myself
And while you tried to free me
I still can't free myself
And while you want to be with me
I still can't be myself

SUMMON ME

Summon me in the dark
Dance in circles and sing
Chant nonsense
Summon me in the dark
Not with crudely drawn runes
Chalk pentagrams
Symbols with no names
But with empty glasses
Bottles to the dregs
Good stories
Better laughter
Hastily assembled gifts of love
Burnt offerings of support
The scent of life well lived lingering in the air
Summon me in the dark
So you might bring me to the light

DESTROY ERASE IMPROVE

The creative process
Is evolution
Constantly inconsistent
Regularly irregular
Dependably changing and erratic
It strengthens as time passes
It makes mistakes
Misses that send it backwards
But always growing always learning
Success builds on success
And failure breeds a lesson
The creative process
Is evolution
We create
We destroy
We improve
And we do it over
And over and over
Again

MISTAKES

The only thing I've ever made of my life
Is mistakes
The only thing I've ever made of myself
More mistakes
Every day every action every inaction
Mistake after mistake
Every lesson learned every one ignored
Just mistakes
Is it regret
Is it pain
Are these things just more mistakes
Second guesses and instinctive action
It all seems to be mistakes
Accidental or deliberate
I only seem capable
Of mistakes

THIS IS CYNICAL

Have you discovered the meaning of life?
The point of living?
Clearly it is working
Hard
Working
Long
To attempt to save
To build
A future you may never see
The point of living is not the now
Not today
Not this moment
It's the tomorrow
The day that never comes
Break your backs for it
Crack their whips for it
Fingers to the bone for it
Do not enjoy the now
The present
This moment
It is nothing
No
The meaning of life
Is for tomorrow and the next day
Maybe you'll get there
To enjoy it

BACK IN MY MIND

Sitting in this chair
Staring as the paint chips
Feeling so heavy
Im watching as the air drips
Im stuck in it now
With no where to go
Im stuck in it now
With no where to go
Im stuck in it now
The only thing I know
Is
Running away from the back of my mind

Im running away
From the back of my mind
Running away from the back of my mind

Im running away
From what's back in my mind

AN ATTEMPT

Just sit
I tell myself
How hard can it be
Sit
Lean back
Close your eyes
And just be

I take a deep breath
Try to push it all away
Just sit
But my eyes are darting back and forth
Beneath their lids
My ears prickle
Every sound amplified
My mind my mind my mind
Races thinking evaluating doubting
Just sit
My tendons tighten
My fingers ache to grip something
My legs tense up
My whole body is against me

Just sit

Just be

Just exist

For a moment

Stop
And just be

How hard
Could
That
Be

SUMMER FRUIT

I remember the summer days
The windows down
Side by side
Wind blown
Wandering
Restlessly and endlessly

I remember the summer evenings
Your hand on mine
Ice in the drinks
Rum in the glasses
Side to side
Talking
Senselessly and endlessly

I remember the summer nights
Your lips on mine
Sweat on the sheets
Skin to skin
Together
Ravenously and endlessly

I remember the summers

TELL THE WORLD

Learn to tell the world
FUCK YOU
From time to time
You've earned the right
To silence
To peace
To quiet
To tell the world
Leave me the FUCK ALONE
I do NOT want to participate
I am NOT here for your entertainment
I am NOT here to prove myself to you
I am here to live
To be
To exist
And to make of that what I will
Learn to tell the world
FUCK YOU
Leave
Me
Be

WITCH TRIAL

Execution
I'm tattooed to the stake
The pyre burns
A witch trial
Mine
My own
The faces look up
Mine
My own
The face screaming out in fear
Mine
My own
No breaking the bonds
No extinguishing the flames
I am tattooed to the stake
My hands bound
By my hand
Sentenced to death
I am the judge
I am the jury
I am the hooded executioner
And I
Shall burn

STORM-WORN LOVER

It was a dark and stormy night
In the mind of one lost lover
Drifting through the wind and rain
Trying to discover
Why his heart had gone so far
Wandered from its other
Now out alone and cold
Exposed without its cover
No warm embrace to keep it safe
The flames of passion it had smothered
And now he wanders all alone
This lost and lonely lover

LIE

The best lie I ever told
Was when I was just nineteen
I told myself this world
Was beautiful and free
I told myself that I could be
Anything I've ever dreamed
I told myself I could be happy
And that I'd know what that would mean
But it was all a beautiful lie
Hideous and ugly
No matter how hard I tried
I just couldn't find the ending of this
Poem.

MONSTERS

When I look in the mirror
I look for the monsters
I look for the beast
I look for the ravager
I look for the betrayer
The destroyer
The usurper
The user
The abuser
The sinner
I search my eyes
The shadows beneath them
I search my scars
The sins behind them
The hollowness
The emptiness
I look for the monsters
Staring straight back at me

DO I CREATE OR DESTROY

One hand creates
One hand destroys
But I'm not ambidextrous
So I put them together
Under my chin
And formulate the words
And write
Creation from destruction
Destruction from creation
Disassembling myself
Reconstructing myself
Salvation in destruction
Damnation in creation
I put my hands together
Pen between
And I write

SO MUCH GIVEN SO MUCH WASTED

Every single one of us is trying to survive
Everything around us is trying to thrive

But we are not thriving
Barely surviving
And really just fucking dying
Pathetic how little we're actually trying
Running in circles buying and buying
Kicking and screaming crying and crying

What a waste with so little drive
I wonder if we could even revive.

TO DIE FOR

Give me something to die for
Something to strive for
Something to thrive for
Something to drive toward

Give me a reason to be reckless
A reason to be senseless
A reason to be defenseless
A reason to be a complete mess

Give me something to
Aspire for
Expire for
Desire for
Light this world on fire for
Give me something to die for

PROSE: ABOUT JUNE 2023

Last December/I exposed myself/
to those closest to me/I discovered myself
and revealed myself/pan-sexual/
and so far I've been/hesitant/contemplative/
anxious/about pride month/
would I show myself/beyond myself/I don't know
that I've ever been/proud/of anything I
am/but I am at least learning/
to hate myself/a little less/every day.

YOU, AGAIN

I miss you
I miss you in ways that goddamn hurt
I miss you in ways that make me a fool
I miss you in ways that make me want to
Scream
I miss you in ways that make me
Cry
I miss you in timeless ways of old
I miss you in brand new ways
I miss you every day
Every moment
Every kind of way
I miss you
And I know its only my fault

LIVE - TO - LIVE

You don't just get to choose
Not to live
You do
You don't just get to choose
Not to participate
You exist
You don't just get to float by
You act
Life happens to us all
You live
Life happens in every moment
You exist
Choices are made in every moment
You do
Or you don't
But you do
You are a part of this
Embrace it

MUSE

Is my muse
Desolation?
Desperation?
Am I only able to create
When misery consumes me?
Do I love my depression?
Do I love my self-loathing?
Have I ever really tried
To put myself back together?
Am I capable of creating
Joy?
Happiness?
Or only
Pain
And sadness?
What does my muse
Say about me?

I AM NO WOLF

I am trapped by the past
Shackled to it
I want so badly to be free
But lack the conviction
To chew through my own leg

GREAT EXPECTATIONS

They told me I was gifted
I was special
I'd be great
They told me I was skilled
I'd go far
I'll amaze
They said I was charming
I was outgoing
I was smart
They heaped on the compliments
The attributes
The expectations
They gave me special classes
Special work
Special roles
They gave me lofty visions
Higher standards
Bigger goals
They gave me spotlights
When I didn't want to be seen
They gave me no help
When I asked for assistance
They gave me stricter rules
Harder jobs
Longer days

They gave me special speeches
Harder critique
A firmer hand
They gave me harsher words
Meaner looks
More sever punishments
They gave me classmates who competed
Peer vs peer
They gave me isolation
Me vs dreams
Loftier the goals
More brutal the failure
More unacceptable the misstep
They gave me myself
The most difficult of critic
They gave me doubt
And fear
And self-loathing
And disappointment
They gave me unreachable expectation
And settled for nothing less
They said I was gifted
They said I'd be great
They said I'd excel
They said I could do it
All on my own
They said I was special

Why did I fail?

YOUTH

My youth is gone
Used up and wasted
Do not recycle
Tossed in the trash
With empty bottles
Crumpled cans
Dregs of spent ashtrays
The dirt it tracked in, swept up and dumped
The tissues that dried tears
And the bandages that dried blood
Used up with reckless abandon
My youth is gone
And I want for it

GUNS

It's guns
Guns
Guns
Guns
The problem
Is guns
Not immigration
Not self-expression
Not gender identity
Not mental health issues
Guns
Access to guns
Having guns
Owning guns
Worshiping guns
Prioritizing guns
Buying and selling guns
You fucking imbeciles
The problem
Is fucking
Guns

SLEEP

Sometimes
All I want to do is sleep
Seek that embrace of
Nothingness

But i'm not any good at it
I'm a typhoon
A storm of restlessness
Endless writhing
Twisting and turning
A mind always bounding
And a body never still

Sometimes
All I want to do is sleep
Just one more way
I let myself down

PROPAGATION OF PAIN

The propagation of pain
Throughout my body
Like waves
Crashing into rocky walls
Staggering
Powerful
Awesome

As if
The world were shattering
Pain in my mind
Exploding
Like a billion points
Of far off light

And now
Too late
The realization
The sensation

No mitigation
Of this propagation
Of pain

REFLECTION

I know it's me
On the other side of the mirror
But when I stare
When I look deep
I do not recognize
Me anymore
Who I've become
Who I've been
The choices I've made
The things that I've done
All have my name signed
I know it's me
It can't be anyone else
But I don't
Recognize me anymore

PERSUASIVE DEMONS

My demons
Oh so persuasive
Ring through my brain
My heart
My gut
Demons of the night
Of the days
The waking hours
The sweetest dreams
My demons
Oh so persuasive
They whisper
I listen
They point
I go
My demons
My demons
Oh, so persuasive
I wish to resist
Just once.

SHADOWS

The streetlight flicks on
Illuminating the side of the house
Creating shadows
As the wind bellows on
Shaking the trees from side to side
Moving shadows
As the window rattles on
Echoing from one side to another
Disturbing shadows

I watch it all from under my eyes
Catching shadows

CARBON COPY

Is anyone an original
Anymore?
Is there anything left
To say first
Think first
Feel first
Do first
Or has it really
All been done
Before?

Perhaps
Much more important
Does not being first
Mean it isn't sincere?

I am not the first to love
But that does not mean
I cannot
Love the most.

FTP (ANGER)

Fuck the police
Fuck the power

Fuck the murder and the violence and the abuse

Fuck the bloodshed the death
Fuck the badges fuck the immunity
Fuck the shootings
Fuck the pensions

Fuck the power
Fuck the police

BLEEDING FAILURE

There come moments
When even rejection
Feels like success
You've failed again
Cut yourself open and bled again
Nothing to show
Nothing for all your hard work
Save a letter
Brief
Thank you we're not interested
And you feel elated
Just for a second
Because at least
You tried

PASSING LANE

This too shall pass
They say
Again
And again
This, too, shall pass
But when everything that passes
Is followed by something new
We must wonder
What we're waiting for
To pass
Is it these seemingly never ceasing
Instances
Or is it
Life itself
That someday, too
Will pass

A PHONE CALL

My Dad just called
He regularly does
He asked me what was new
Nothing I said nothing with me
Tell me what's new with you
Small daily stories
Good and bad news
Rarely a thing of significance
But it is never about the conversation,
No,
It is simply about the relationship

SO WHAT

Nicotine
Caffeine
Amphetamines
Blah blah blah
So what it rhymes
So what there's grime
So what there's slime
On this life of mine
Im fucking fine
Read the signs
I might be dyin'
I might be fightin'
I might be strivin'
I might be lyin'
Blah blah blah
Gimme more

WHEN I WAS YOUNG

When I was young
I only knew
How to write
Anger &
Sadness
Pain defined me
Fear confined me
I never expressed anything else

Now that I'm older
I only want
To write
About growth &
Change
Fear drives me
Pain inspires me
But I still don't know anything else

STRESS

It clouds my mind
Obscures my sight
Restricts my ability to act
Everything feels tense
Tight
Wound up
Every movement feels spring-loaded
Immobilized by indecision
Everything blends together
A cacophony of existence
Swirls around my head
I'm stressed
Again.

TICK/TOCK

The calendar is a lie
A construct
A restriction placed upon ourselves
By ourselves
The hours days months weeks seconds
Of your life
Do not exist
Erosion is real
Entropy is reality
Your age is a lie
Time is
If a lobster can live forever
Immortal
Then so can we

UNWILLINGLY RETURNED

Do you ever wonder
What resurrection
Feels like?

Death is a release
Relief
An end
And then
It all is forced back into you

Life goes on
After dreams come true
Now what?

Resurrection
Is it a reward
Or is it for those who didn't
Get it right the first time?

THE CREEPING THINGS

I fear the creeping things
But I love them
For the weirdness
Makes me feel
Hopeful
Whole
Emboldened
I fear the weirdness
I fear the dark
I fear the silence
I fear my own heart
I love the creeping things
For their darkness
Makes me feel
Known.

DEPRESSION, AD NAUSEAM

How to explain
How hard it is
To do a simple thing
How much effort it can take
To send a text message
To make dinner
To watch a movie
To wake up
To not be asleep
To have the desire
But be unable to stir your own body
How hard it is
To simply live

HUNTER HAUNTED

I run from the horrors that chase me
But they follow
They hunt
Mistakes
Traumas
Abuse
I run
They chase
They hunt
So I turn
I face them
They give pause
Now I hunt them
I hunt the horrors
I hunt the dark
I chase
In circles
Eternally
We run

A POEM I WROTE IN HIGH SCHOOL # 1

My soul is starved
For attention
For affection
Dying and drying up into nothing
Lacking the love
It needs to thrive
Lacking the will
It needs to survive
Drowning itself in sadness
Burning and burying itself in madness
Killing me by extension

WISDOM OF PARENTS

You listen to me you little shit
You piece of shit
You waste of time
Worthless piece of shit
Never amount to anything
Unteachable unreachable
Keep your mouth shut don't backtalk
You do what I say
Don't think
You worthless little fuck

MY BRAIN

My brain is tired
It just wants sleep
But my body won't stop
Moving
Shaking
Twitching
Shivering
Shuddering
Quaking
Running off energy
From an imaginary source
My mind wants peace
My body is at war
I just want to sleep

OBSCENE AS HEARTBREAK

I'm on my knees
Praying to the mirror
Begging begging begging
For it to end
For forgivness
Begging to be free
As I feel it grow inside me
Ripping
Tearing
Its way deeper
Begging for it to stop
As it consumes me
From within

INSIDE ME

I am sick
I feel unwell
Somethings wrong
Inside of me

I can't see it
But I feel it
Somethings wrong
Inside of me

I am sick
I feel wrong
Somethings off
Inside of me

I can't tell what
But I feel it

DRIEW

Weird is a way
For attention to get
With orders and words
Jumbled and mixed

Not as you seem
Things out of order
Flowing all wrong
Lines outside the border

Forthwards and back
Sounds all odd
Reason and rhyme
Are just gone

LIFE (CRAZY HOW IT WORKS)

Does it ever amaze you
That things
Work as well as they do?
Spinning through the cosmos
On a ball of heat and dust
Life an instance
A marvel and amazement unparalleled
Success
And yet
Pure rage when the WiFi is down

TO BE ALRIGHT

I wonder what its like
To feel alright
To have your head in the clouds
Not fear the ground
To be uplifted
Gifted
Not care that time's sand shifted
To be with the breeze
Be calm and at ease
I wonder what its like
To just be alright

APARTMENTALIZED

I would never leave
My apartment
If I could.

There is safety in isolation
That outweighs any bit
Of loneliness.

Safety from pain
Not that which would be inflicted on me
By others
But that which would be inflicted on others
By me.

GONE

Gods not here
Even if they ever were
Long gone now
Bad parent
Absentee
Abandoned all creation
Left us to our devices
Gave us good will
Evil intentions
Left us behind
Gods not here
Humanity is
That scares me enough

INFLUENCE & HONESTY

I don't want to be famous
For the sake of fame
It sounds like a real pain in the ass
I just want
An opportunity
To make people see
Whatever they feel
They're not the only one
Never alone
Also, the money sounds good.

THE SILENT JUDGE

What secrets can you discern
Just by looking me over
What shame can you discover
Just passing me by
What horrors can you uncover
Just watching me leave
What things can you learn
Just judging silently

JUST LET ME DO IT LATER

I'll write later
I'll clean later
I'll do the dishes later
I'll cook later
I'll think later
I'll feel later
i'll cry later
I'll try to come to grips later
I'll try to be okay later
I'll do it all later
For now just leave me be
Just let me do it later

I WANT TO WRITE A POEM

I think I'm going
To write a poem
I'll use words
A rhyme
A rhythm
Images and colors
I think I'm going
To write a poem
I'll inject pain
Memories
It will inspire
You to feel
I think
Im going
To write
A poem
Maybe.

LIES OF THE REPUBLIC

Don't tell me it's for our own good
Don't say it's out of love
It's not for our protection
Or because you care
Say it's because of fear
Tell me it's for control
Admit it's so you can own us
Mind & body & soul

MEDIA OF A SOCIAL NATURE

Don't let social media
Lie
To you
Everyone else's life sucks too
Everyone else's world is full of shit
Everyone hurts
Everyone struggles
Everyone cries
Some just *take cool pictures* while they do

BREATHING ASH

I take a deep breath
To breath in this new air
And I choke
On the ashes of the past
But I think I like
The asphyxiation
A sharp reminder
That what is past is never gone
That what is finished
Is never done

COMPREHEND THE NIGHT

I cannot comprehend
The endlessness of night
So pure and powerful
The complete lack of light
Gazing up towards worlds
Entirely out of sight
Terrors staring back at me
And endless source of fright

SELF-LOVE

I hate the sound of my own voice

Even in my head
I hate the sight of my own face
Even in my head
I hate the way I speak and act
Even in my head

I can't escape these things I hate

Even in my head

BONES BELOW

Step on my broken bones
Strewn across the floor
Bare foot
Feel the sharp points
The jagged edges
The pain of my pain
My soul in your sole
Step on my broken bones
And tread into your future

TALKING TO THE
REARVIEW MIRROR

Turn back
I begged
We were going to fast
Turn back
I begged
Sirens cried out behind
Turn back
I begged
Everything was coming apart
Don't worry
He said
This roads a dead end

PARASITE

I am
The parasite

One life
Isn't enough
I've found

I need
Another

More
To feed on
To drain
To suck
To dry

More
Another

One life
Isn't enough

I am
The parasite

YOU

Ask me what I want
And I'll say
I don't know
Ask me what I need
And I'll say
Nothing
Ask me what I'm missing
And I'll say
Something
Ask me what it is
And I'll say
You

THINGS I HEARD GROWING UP

Man up
Don't be a bitch
Suck it up
No pain no gain
Don't be a pussy
You're weak
Don't cry
Or I'll give you something to cry about
You wuss
You're pathetic
Be a man

COUCH

Yeah…

I'm depressed
I must admit it

I lay on this couch
Getting fatter
Feeling sadder

I should be madder
At myself

I did this
To myself

I'm depressed
I must admit it

TREASURE

I had it all
But gave it up
For less I thought was more

And now in solitude I sit
Happier alone
Than pretending to replace

The irreplaceable

FEEL

I can't make you understand it
If you don't understand it
How I feel.
And that's okay
It's better this way
I'd rather you not feel
How I feel.

GIVE EM' HELL

Live your life
Become ungovernable
Be the solution
That is part of the problem

Stand up
Speak out
Fight back
And give 'em hell

CHURCH CLOTHES

Put on something nice
Its Sunday
Dress well
Show off
Careful of the mud
Though you're being buried
In your church clothes

DRUGS @ 3AM

Everything
Is
A
Downer
If you think
About
The fact
That
We're taking them
To feel
Better
Than we
Can
On
Our
Own

A SIMPLE POEM

This is a simple poem
A simple notion
Clear emotion
A straightforward motion
How it goes is:
Fuck transphobic bullshit

SINS

Of all
The sins
To cross
My lips
You
Were the
Sweetest

Of all
The lies
To cross
My hips
You
Were the
Meanest

WHISKEY SOUR

You'd look nice with some whiskey in you.

The words trailed her as she walked out the door
leaving it open as to invite a fleeting glance
one last look as she vanished

But I resisted
and had a drink

WHAT-IF HEART

What if the sun stole its light from the moon
What if the stars went dark
That's what it feels like
Without you in my heart

HIDDEN

Not all strength
Is physical
Not all pain
Is visible
Not all weakness
Is dismissible
Not all battles
Are winnable

HAPPY AS A CLAM

When I'm not open
The guilt eats me up
So I open
And I get what I expected
And it eats me up

AT A PARTY WHEN I WAS 18

I was drunker
She was bigger
I said no
It didn't matter
Ive had erectile dysfunction ever since

LET US STAND

Let us stand unshaken
Unshaken by this changing world
Til' the end of all time
Let us stand unshaken

BEAUTALITY

We must
Brutalize
The norms of society
In order to make great

Art

In order to live great
Lives

ABOUT THE AUTHOR

I have no idea what I'm doing
No idea what to say
All I know is this is me
At least, I am today

EVERYTHING TOO MUCH

Everything just
Feels
Like
Too much
Sometimes.

I guess that's okay.

But it sucks...

QUESTIONS & ANSWERS

Love the questions
Love the search of answers
But don't find them
Leave these spaces blank
And love them for their emptiness

I SAY TO MYSELF

Just let me sit here in peace
I say to myself
Knowing full well
It won't fucking happen

RUINS

Never let me ruin your day
I'm not worth it
Wait
Sorry
I got that backwards.

BRUTAL

One day you'll wake up
You'll realize
You have nothing
And no one is there
To not care

It happens to everyone
It will happen to you.

A HAIKU ABOUT MY PENIS

Oh my dick is small
And it doesn't work that well
Thank you genetics?

DEFEAT?

That's it,
I thought,
As I laid down to die
That's all
That I
Can do

POETRY, AGAIN

Not everything is poetry
But anything
Can be

BRUTALITY ROMANTACIZED

I hate myself
But
I think I'm
In love
With that

CRSH ND BRN

I imagined being myself
Just for a day.
The waking up was *misery*

INKY BLACK

When my ink
Runs dry
I stab my heart
And write
In blood
And pain

SHINY RED BALLOON

I've given up telling you
I miss you
I'm sick of hearing the words echo around
The emptiness of your absence

But I do.

(NO) SUICIDE NOTE PT 1

Selfishly
One of the worst parts
Is never knowing
If breaking your heart
Was part of why you did it

A FOUR LETTER EMOTION

And then...
Just like that
It stopped.

And then
Just like that...
It started again.

And then
Just like that
I felt everything...

AND I NEVER LEARN

If there is a way
To fail
I will find it
Like a pathfinder
A way-finder
A divining rod of fucking up
Watch what I do
And run the opposite way

ARTIST ISN'T EXCLUSIVE

As an artist you need to believe you are
Exception
You must also be
Delusional
Imaginative
A little bit eccentric
Erratic
Haunted
And traumatized
Overly sensitive
Overly stimulated
You need to believe the impossible
That you can succeed where others cannot
That you can see what others cannot
That you can be what others cannot
You need to be
All of this.
Or none of it.

We are all creators.

HOLD UP, WAIT A MINUTE

Let me stop right here for a second
Before I go on
'Working on myself'
And
'Mending my trauma'
Is there anyone who likes me
The way I am?
…
Okay then
Back to our regularly scheduled struggle

NOT POETIC JUST TRUE

I'm so tired of feeling
Stressed
Depressed
Anxious
Unrest
I just want to feel
Something
Anything
Any way
Different

PENNY FOR MY THOUGHTS

There's a sign
Spray painted on plywood
Propped up against my brain
Yard Sale
Everything must go!
$1 OBO

There are no buyers

Stuck with this –
With these
Never ceasing thoughts

GIVE UP GIVING UP

I don't want to give up
I've just grown so tired
Of the taste of failure
Its flavor has soured my tongue
And now even success tastes wrong

ENERGY (ADHD)

I'm all energy
Unfocused
Unrestrained
Unrestricted
Uncontrolled
Unproductive

It's there
The energy

But it is useless to me
Like a hamster wheel
Going
Nowhere

FAT AND OLD

My body is a horrid thing
Fat and stretched
Flabby and weak
Aged and aging
Joints crack
Muscles hardly there
Tendons threatening to snap
A physical representation
Of the great failure
That is I

EXECUTION

This is what I do
On the night of my heart's execution
I cling to the pyre
I cling to the crucifix
I cling to the gallows
For any last
Lingering
Touch
Of you

I USED TO CUT MYSELF
NOW I JUST BREAK MY HEART

This wound
It is a gift
In reverse
It starts opened wide
And slowly will heal in time
Turning into wrapped flesh
A scar
Like a holiday ribbon
Twisted artfully around the memory
Of the wound
Self-inflicted

MOVING BOXES

Moving boxes
Stacked in my mind
Half-filled
Destination unknown
Contents forgotten

I can't keep packing these thoughts up
Hoping someone takes them away

NOT QUITE BULLETPROOF

What makes you think
This will work
I say to myself
As I dip my hand
Into the machine gun fire of your heart
I refuse to give up
Just because
I'm shot full of holes

POETRY, REDUX

A collection of words
A selection of rhymes
A dedication of minds
Slit my throat
Let the words flow
Sticky wet and crimson
Enjoy them at this conclusion

SELF PORTRAIT

This is me
A shattered man
Stones I threw
A tattered man
Winds I blew
A battered man
Blows I knew
This is me
My own creation

SMELLS LIKE GUNPOWDER

Where there was a voice
In my head
There is now only the empty hollow
Echo
Of a gun shot
And the lingering smell
Of abandonment

SOME THINGS ARE
POETIC IN NATURE

I lay on the couch
And watch a movie
Alone
And think of you

THE ATTIC

The footsteps in the attic
Were much more than I had thought
Ghostly steps that led through memories
And your fingerprints on my heart

THE REGRETFUL THIEF

I stole from you
I stole from me
The greatest thing
I'll ever know

I robbed myself
Of everything

I took away
Everything

I want it back
I want to give it back

But the last thing I deserve
Is another chance

UNSPOKEN VOLUMES

I know so many words
And yet none can describe
How my heart aches

I suppose that's why
I have tears

VENOM VOICED

Snakes
Coil inside me
A nest of vipers
Waiting to strike
Anything sweet that draws near
My voice is their venom
Poisoning fools who approach
And I am alone
With my snakes

WASN'T READY

I wasn't ready to say goodbye
I never thought I'd have to

I wasn't ready to let you go
I always thought I'd have you

THIS POEM IS ABOUT DEPRESSION

The beast came back for me
It ran me down in the pale light of late-night tv
Stalked me through the forest of empty cans
And fast food soda cups
It hunted me through the miasma of mess
Ruins built of dirty laundry cast aside
Pounced on me while I slept
Half buried under the rubble of blankets in the
Couch-shaped casket I laid
The beast pounced upon me
Sunk its fangs deep in
And the venom began to spread
From my head to my hands to my feet
It had me again. This time I didn't even struggle to
Escape.

ATLAS HELD THE HEAVENS

Some days I am triumphant
Some days its all I can do
To keep the sky from falling in on me

Some days I crumble

But some days
I don't

ALL THESE THINGS I'VE COST MYSELF

I love you
I hope your day is going well
I hope you have a good evening
I hope you sleep well
I hope you dream well
I hope the sun shines on you when you wake
I love you
From a distance
Because I stole away
My own right
To stand right next to you
To lay right beside you
And say
I love you

AND YOUR LIPS ARE HEAVEN

Your hips are a purgatory from which
I never
Want to escape

BLEEDING INK

Sharpened pen
Like a blade
I jabbed it into my wrist
And bled these words
Bleeding ink
Into the pages
Bare it all
Through open wounds

CAN'T FALL IF YOU DON'T GET UP

My depression runs my life
Like some kind of overbearing foreman
Micro-managing yet negligent at the same time
Only stepping in when things start to go well
To push them back off track
As long as I'm down things are fine
When I start to climb up is when I get shoved
Down again
Then it hurts all over
And begs the question,
Why not just stay down?

CAN'T TRUST GOOD THINGS

Why so anxious
When good things come
Why so resistant
Why so hesitant

Because good things
Never lasted
No,
Good things
Aways got
Taken away.

CHIMERA

I'm a monstrosity
I am pain and darkness
Anguish and anxiety
Stubborn and weak
A hideous mixture of faults
Self-absorbed and self-loathing
Deadly combinations of emotions
I am humanity
A true monstrosity

DEPRESSION INFINITE

The day hasn't ended
But I need it to
I don't know what to do
With myself
My mind
My body
I just wait
For the days to end

DEPRESSION, YET AGAIN

I haven't gone anywhere today
Haven't walked anywhere
Haven't traveled anywhere today
I haven't even taken a shower
Scrubbed off the week of work and sweat
And exhaustion
Yesterday's anxiety clings in my hair
Yesterday's stress clings to my pits
Yesterday's tee shirt sticky in the heat
Is it laziness
Is it depression

I'll hold it against myself either way

HAPPY THOUGHTS?

I feel like I should be dead
And I wonder why I'm not
Because I cling to life
Or life clings to me
I've no desire to go on
But my subconscious seem to know better
And so
I feel like I should be dead
And I wonder why I'm not

I WONDER

What could I be
If I let go
Of everything
I was

WASTED PAGES

Am I even any good at this
Is there really any point
Do I just fill pages with words
Words never to be read
Pages to die in silence and obscurity
Pages unfulfilled
Pages wasted
Is it selfish of me to use so many words
What if language is a finite resource
Ive squandered so much of it
Ive wasted so many pages

WORDS ARE JUST WORDS
UNTIL YOU DIE TO THEM

Child of Avalon
Rebel of Babylon
Scion of Megatron
This is your life
This is your death
This is your strife
This is your breath
Shed tears of joy
Shed cries of pain
Shed blood of woes
Shed skin of shame
Child of Babylon
Rebel of Avalon
This is your life

WON'T GET OUT ALIVE

My memories have teeth
Bared barbed and bloody
Sinking into my neck
Ripping away my protective flesh
Exposing the bloody pulp of my inner self
My vulnerability
I am a feast for my memories
At their mercy
Never to escape

THE FIRE DIED

Tense every muscle in my body
Til it aches
To the point that they'll break
Coiled like iron
And then
I walk in the fire
Breath in the heat
Step through the coals
Ash all around
I've extinguished my soul

THE CURE IS THE POISON

Can't I be happy with
What I am
What I have
How I look
No.
Is it my fault?
Or is it society?
Either way
I hate myself
So I'll stress eat another cheeseburger

STUCK ON REPEAT

I've made mistakes
I'll make again
Like a song on repeat
I know the words by heart now
I know each note
It's as if I'm one with the music now
I've heard it so often
And so it is with my missteps
My mistakes
I've made them
I'll make them again

REGRETFULLY MINE FOREVER

They died
I buried them
But one by one they claw their way
Out of the grave
And back into my skull
Each mistake
Each regret
Resurrected by my inability to forgive
My refusal to forget
Undead they claw through my mind
Into my heart
And dig new graves
Forever with me

P A N S E X U A L

Letting out my identity
Was a slow process
Like dragging a blade
A broken shard of glass
A sharpened stone
Down my arm
The blood red truth slowly
Seeping out
More and more as I went
Becoming easier
Until the cut was elbow to wrist
And I was bled of truth and identity

MY HEART PUMPS SALT

Salt my wounds
Salt my earth
You never were here
You never were here

LIKE GETTING LOST
IN A GOOD BOOK

You were my favorite story
I loved to get lost in your words
Find myself wandering
From page to page
Across your lips across your skin
Memorizing each word as I went

Now I can close my eyes
And recall passages
Recall moments recall lines
But the joy the comfort
Is replaced with a ravenous
Longing

JUST BREATHE

Deep breath
Inhale the world around me
Hold it in
Feel it swell in my lungs
Slowly expel it back out
Changed now by me
In this simple moment
I've reshaped part of the world

IMMOLATE ME

You lit the match
And dropped in on me
I did not know
I was covered in gasoline
And now the flames have erupted
And I am consumed
Flames of passion
I am burning at your hand

ITS LIKE THAT

I live my life
Inside a pit
Surging black and deep
Endless
And continuously
I fall

LIVE YOUR DEATH
TO THE FULLEST

Life
Is a death sentence
The instant we're born the clock starts to tick
Are we ever really alive?
Do we ever really live?
Or are we simply pretending
Playing at life
When really all we are
Is dying
From the onset

LIKE A PACK OF WOLVES

My words
My words my words my words
Chomping at my throat
From the inside
Aching to tear their way out
Splatter on this page
And run towards the margins
Leaving bloody footprints
For you to read along the way

LIPS

Every place your lips touched my body
Is turned to a scar
I cherish them all

CURIOSITY KILLS

Death makes me curious
What's on the other side
I want to know
To see
But fear
I'll like it even less
Than this plain life

DREAMS IN THE MACHINE

When did we give up on our dreams?
Let them go from our desperate grasp
To shrivel up
Dry up and curl in
Browning and flowerless and turn to rot
Amidst the pile in the corner
Forgotten as they decay
Molded to a dusty filthy grey.
Dispose of your dreams here
Place your hopes in the designated bins
Compost your future your potential your talents
Allow them to decay and fall apart
Unfulfilled dreams creating piles of ranking refuse
Devoid of hope sapped of power
Not nurturing the ground for the seeds of future
dreams
Nothing will be planted for others
Crushed to uselessness in a stubborn grip
Drop them in the waste
And move along
Shuffled forward
Please do not slow or stop keep the line moving
Leaving wants and desires behind

Don't look back
Move ahead move ahead move ahead
You failed your dreams so throw them away and
Blindly walk on
Join the hoard of others just the same
The body is fine keep it moving keep it working
Keep the wheel turning

Dreamers do not fuel the machine

Dreamers do not run the machine

Dreamers *simply do not.*

COSMIC HORROR

I know why people want to believe in gods
It's comforting
Compared to the truth
The fact that we're all here by accident
No great design
No fate
No seers spinning threads of destiny
Just collisions of dust
In endless space
It's a horrifying truth
I'd seek comfort too
If I were too afraid to face it

BLOODY REBELLION

I beg my heart to let go
But it refuses
It clings it longs it yearns
Militant in its dedication
As if my want to move on
Were an oppression
It's beats act of rebellion in a fight
My own heart
Like a rebel fighting for freedom
Against me
But all I want is freedom from
The memories

A VERY BAD RYHME

I think about when I was young
All the things I could have done
All the times I wanted none
None of it.
All the bullshit. All the pain.
All the trauma that I gained.
All I lost all that was taken.
I thought I was okay but I was mistaken.
And now here I am
An old sad amalgam
Of all the shit I waded through
All the garbage that made me who
I am today but at what cost
If I weren't me what would be lost?
Oh well. Oh well.
Oh well again.
It's over it's done with and that's
Something.

2024 FLOW

New year
Same me
Same face
Same days
Same disgrace
Same mistakes
Same displaced mess
Unrest and yet mediocre at best
Same failure
Same claims to hail your
Self-doubt and disdain
Same things I can claim
Same shit on my brain
Same chems in my veins
Still the same me I'll always be
Be it 2024 or 2023
New year new day new place new tastes
No
Rinse repeat and rinse repeat and rinse
I've been this person forever since
I'll die this person despite my best
Efforts to change its a loosing game
I could complain
But fuck it
Happy new year

"HOME"

My apartment is a reflection of my mind
Cluttered yet empty
Needing to be cleaned but not a disaster
Comforting but hollow
Familiar but strange
It is protective shelter and restrictive prison
The only place I want to be
And the place I want to leave the most

A BROKEN NEON TUBE

Like the signs that bleed their neon
Into the rain soaked streets
My heart seeps endlessly
A stream of anguish
From what was once a source of love

A TASTING

I am
My own
Worst
Everything

ALL OF IT

A ghost only has
As much power as you give it
So ask yourself
How much power
Do you give
To the things that haunt you
To the past

BE LIKE BRICKS
THROUGH WINDOWS

Throw a brick through the consciousness
Of humankind

Shatter

Beliefs
Notions
Concepts

Wreck

The process
The illusion
The simulation

Be the brick
With a note tied around it
We will not suffer you any longer

Shatter

the consciousness of humankind

BLIND TO THEM

Why would I leave my demons behind?
Put them in position to sneak up
Attack from the back
Knives and teeth
No,
I won't leave my demons behind me
I would rather keep them in my sight

CLOUD COVER

I don't write enough
Words spill from my mind
Hit the paper with force
Soak into the pages
Flooding the lines
Torrential

But it isn't enough
I live in drought
The pages still thirst
They still yearn for drink
Unslakable

There's just not enough
The clouds gather
But at best they obscure
Instead of raining down
Stratus

CONSEQUENTIAL

You are the consequence
Of choices
Made by people you've never met
At times when you were never alive

GHOST

Let me in
To haunt your soul
I won't move things around
Or take up any space
I'll hardly make a sound
But you'll know I'm there

HOW THE MIGHTY...

I fall too easily
As if every step I take
Were on an icy precipice
Over a deep chasm of emotion
Of feeling
And sickly sweet winds whip at my face
Tug at my arms and legs
While I struggle futilely to keep balance
I never have a chance
I fall
So easily

I

I cannot love myself
I do not have the capacity
I will never forgive myself
I do not have the ability
I won't ever stop loving you
I'll never run out of eternity
I won't stop missing you
I don't deserve that serenity

HOME IS WHERE THE HAUNT IS

One day
We will haunt this place
Together

I MISS MY FRIENDS: FOR J & R & K

I miss the days of friends
Of staying up late together
Sleeping in together
Wandering the neighborhood just to see
Who was home
I miss the days of 'home' being a blurry concept
Between houses and families
Of having people to care about
And people to care about me
About the mundane troubles of youth
I miss the long phone calls
The long afternoons of doing nothing
The shared victories the shared defeats
The bitter jealousy of someone liking your girlfriend
The endless joy of leaving school and starting a
Weekend together
Of summer vacation
I miss movie theaters and road trips and
Video arcades
And new places and worn-in things
I miss the time of crashing on couches
Sleeping on floors
I miss the groups the dynamics the pairings
I miss the days of friends

HOW MANY TIMES CAN I GIVE UP

I just don't think
I have it in me
Im not cut out for it
Pandering to social media
Endless queries
Constant why bothers
Failing again and again and again
And again
These things I want
Belong to those more deserving
I just don't think
I have it in me

HEAVENLY BODIES

You are the sun
I'm simply the moon
Your radiance
Your warmth
I simply reflect
You are the origin
Of all that is good in me

You are the sun
I am a pale reflection

I DO NOT BELIEVE IN FATE

Eat your fill of destiny
But feel empty still
Fate is an unsatisfactory meal
It will not satiate you
Only leave you wanting for more
Turn away from the table
Make your own
You will find a creation of your own hand
To be much more fulfilling

I'M LIKE A WALKING LIFE LESSON

If you need bad advice
If you need bad decisions
If you need support for poor ideas
If you need someone to make
A fool of yourself with
If you need an example of
All the things not to do
I am here for you

LAUGH THROUGH THE PAIN

Laugh at yourself
Even when no one else will
One voice laughing
Can be enough
To shatter all the world's insecurities

METAPHORICAL TILE

My heart begins to cry
Wracking itself with sobs
Gasps and tears and shaking
Uncontrollably to the point the the sobs
Turn to laughter
Maniacal manic explosive terrifying laughter
No humor just pain
Like a madman crying out in expletive noises
Before it suddenly dies out
Miserable silence

That is how much I miss you.

NO SAFE HARBOR

Where do you turn
When your mind isn't safe
When your own memories
Cause pain
Where can you hide
When inside yourself
Isn't safe

PLAYING WITH GHOSTS

My mind is haunted
And my heart likes to play
When things get darkest
The ghosts come out to play
They've been dead too long
To still be around
But my heart likes to play
And so they survive
When things get darkest
It calls to them
And so my mind is haunted
By ghosts that have been dead
For too long

HOW TO BE YOURSELF

Don't ask me
I surely don't know
I'm still trying
To figure that out
But I think
I think
The secret
Is to just not care
What other people think
Give it a try
Report to me your findings
Im still too insecure
To do it myself

PLEASE JUST FORGET

My mind clings to trauma
And bad memories
Like a drowning man
Clings to oxygen.

RIPTIDE

My mind is a riptide
It pulls me out from under myself
Tosses me about in a sea of
Endless emotion
Drowns me in my own
Anger
Sadness
Failure
Complexity
Complicity
Come and see
Me lost at sea
My mind is the riptide
That swallows me whole

ROCK BOTTOM

I fooled myself
I thought
The healing
Was over
I thought
The sinking was done
I thought I had surfaced
Taken deep breaths
And moved on

But all I had done
Was sink further
To the bottom
Where the light is an illusion
Where the scars bleed anew
I cut my feet on the sharp rocky depths
I think
I found
The bottom

REUNION

I will see you
In the coldest circle of hell
Where the moon
Meets the sun
Where the dark
Becomes light

I will see you
And embrace you like
Death

SEPTEMBER SACRAFICE

Petrichor on leaves and fiery smoke of embers
I'd sacrifice this whole September
If the sacrifice would bring you near
I'd give up the hours give up every day
If only the sacrifice would make you stay

CAT TOY

I hit my head on the floor and my brain fell out
The cat picked it up and dragged it about
Scratched it and kicked it played with and sniffed
it
But ultimately left it behind

So I picked it back up
And shoved it back in
Taped the hole closed
And put myself together again

DEAR EVERYONE, BUT ESPECIALLY YOU

I'm sorry that all I ever did
Was fail you

I wish there was something better
In me.

GOOD LUCK, HE GRINNED

Look at these scars
Each one a tale of
Survival
A hard-fought victory.

Now ask yourself,
If none of this was able to keep me down
What chance do you think you have?

KNOW ME

Love me at my worst
Hate me at my best
See me at my fakest
Know me in my darkest
Trust me at my falsest
Love me at my best

LIFE

I died
Waiting
For myself
To figure it out

PINEAPPLE

Im like a pineapple
A hard spiky exterior
Rough bark
A huge rock hard core that's entirely useless
And a small bit of sweet juicy goodness
That really may not be worth all the trouble

ABOUT THE AUTHOR:

Michael Vlastnik started writing when he was in the 3rd grade and never really stopped. Somewhere along the way he transitioned from being a failed novelist to a poet. His goal with his work has been to provide a window into the struggles that most people face, be it internal or external, and in doing so to hopefully let people know they are not alone in whatever they are going through. This is his 5th, and most personal, collection of poetry. He lives in the pacific northwest with his two cats, who pretend they don't now how to read in order to avoid doing editorial work.

Octave Eight

PUBLISHING

∞